This Walker book
belongs to:

_____ BP

_____

For Lev and Rosie, with bundles of love
A. H.

To my mother bear
L. T.

First published 2016 by Walker Books Ltd
87 Vauxhall Walk, London SE11 5HJ

This edition published 2017

2 4 6 8 10 9 7 5 3 1

Text © 2016 Amy Hest
Illustrations © 2016 Lauren Tobia

The right of Amy Hest and Lauren Tobia to be identified as
author and illustrator respectively of this work has been asserted by them
in accordance with the Copyright, Designs and Patents Act 1988

This book has been typeset in Lasta

Printed in China

British Library Cataloguing in Publication Data:
a catalogue record for this book is available from the British Library

ISBN 978-1-4063-7807-8

www.walker.co.uk

Are You Sure, Mother Bear?

Amy Hest illustrated by Lauren Tobia

WALKER BOOKS
AND SUBSIDIARIES

LONDON • BOSTON • SYDNEY • AUCKLAND

On the first night of winter, it snowed. It snowed and snowed, and Little Miss Bear would not go to sleep. She simply refused.

"Mother Bear!
 Mother Bear!"
she called down the stairs.

"Still no sleep?" her mother
called back. "Not even a wink?"
"It's the snow, Mother. I am
watching the snow!"

Mother Bear sprinkled cinnamon on toast and climbed the stairs and peeked in the room that was yellow. "May I watch, too?" she asked.

"Oh, yes, Mother." Little Miss patted the chair,
and they sat very close in the big purple chair
eating toast. And watching.

Snow covered the garden.
It covered the hills
beyond the garden.

Little Miss and Mother watched for a long time together. From time to time, someone yawned.

"Sleepy, Little Miss?"
"No, Mother. Not even a wink."

"Winter is for sleeping," Mother said.
"But why, Mother?"
"Because that's what bears do," Mother said.
"All bears sleep, all winter long."

"All winter long is much too long." Little Miss put her nose to the window. The stars were bright that night. Little Miss loved the stars.

"I will miss my stars," she said.

"Of course," Mother said. "But your stars will be right there, in their very own place, when we wake up next spring."

"Are you sure, Mother Bear?"
Mother Bear was sure.

The moon was round that night, and hazy. Little Miss loved
the moon. "I will miss my moon," she said.

"Of course," Mother said. "But your moon will be right there,
in its very own place, when we wake up next spring."

"Are you sure, Mother Bear?"
Mother Bear was sure.

Beyond the garden, the snowy hills were especially sparkly that night, just right for rolling. Little Miss loved the hills and rolling. "I will miss my hills," she said.

"Yes," Mother said. "You are very keen on rolling. But your hills will be right there, in their very own place, next spring, for rolling."

"Are you sure, Mother Bear?"
Mother Bear was sure.

Little Miss was sure about something, too. "I want to roll now," she said. "Because I am very keen on rolling."

"Of course," Mother said.

They buttoned blue dressing gowns and pulled on green boots and scarves and mittens.

In the light of the hazy moon, they walked across
the garden.

Shhhuuushhhh went their boots.

Shhhhuuushhhh! Up hills, and down, and up,
to the top of the tallest hill.

The wind blew and their scarves blew ...
and then ...

they rolled!

Over and over they rolled.

Over and over.

Rolling and rolling
in soft snow.

At the bottom of the hill,
they lay very still, watching
the stars and the moon. The sky
in between was blue velvet.

It was time to go home.

Shhhuuushhhh went their boots,
up hills and down, across the garden.

In the room that was yellow, the sheets were cool, the blankets were warm, and Little Miss yawned and yawned.

"Sleepy, Little Miss?"

"No, Mother." And one more yawn.

"Well, good night, Little Miss.
Good night until spring." Mother Bear
kissed the top of her head (like this) ...

and both cheeks (like this) ...

and the tip of her nose
(like this) ... and...

Oh, how Little Miss loved her mother!

"Mother Bear! Mother Bear!" she cried.
"I will miss my Mother Bear!"

"Of course," Mother said, "and I will miss you, too.
But winter is for sleeping. All bears sleep. Even mothers.
And when we wake up, the stars will be bright.
The moon will be round. The hills will be grassy.
And we'll be right here, in our very own place, together."

"Will there be toast?"

"Oh, yes," Mother said. "And after toast, we'll take a little
night walk ... across the garden ... to the top of the tallest
hill ... and then we'll do some *rolling.*"

On the first night of winter, the hills were sparkly with new snow, but Little Miss Bear and her mother were sound asleep. Because winter was here, and that's what bears do.

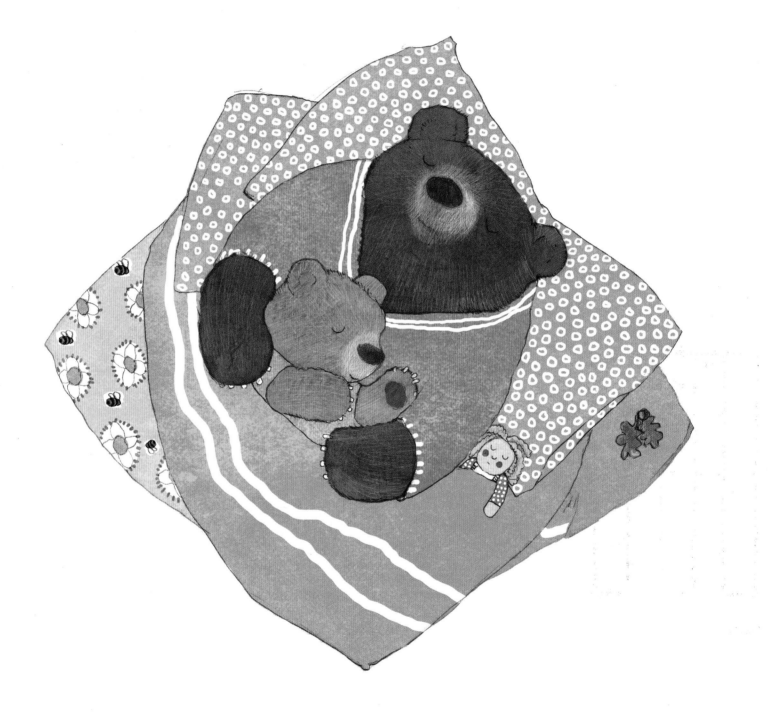